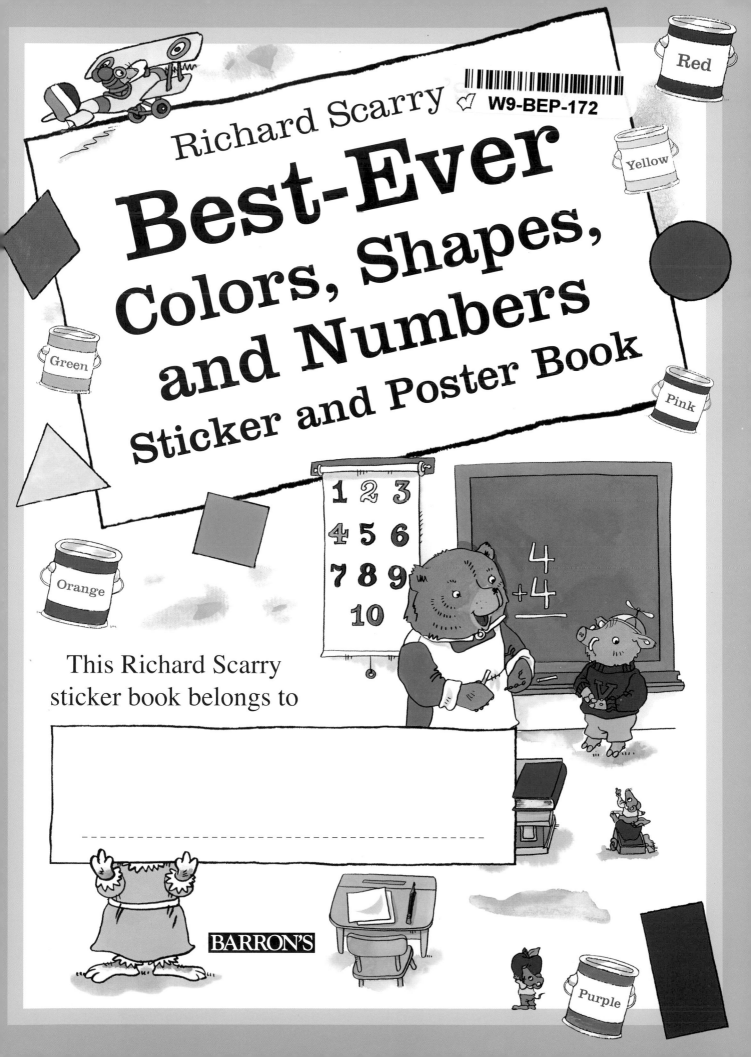

Richard Scarry

Best-Ever
Colors, Shapes, and Numbers
Sticker and Poster Book

Red

Yellow

Green

Pink

Orange

1 2 3
4 5 6
7 8 9
10

This Richard Scarry
sticker book belongs to

Purple

Colorful cars and trucks

Colors make everything bright.
Do you know your colors?
Of course you do!

Orange

Can you see an **orange** dump truck?

Green

What color is Mr. Frumble's pickle car?

Brown

What color is the ice cream on top of the ice cream truck? I wonder what flavor that is?

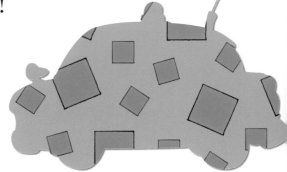

Red
Can you see a **red** fire engine?
Blue
What color is the police car?

Purple
Can you see a **purple** sports car?
Yellow
What color is the garbage truck?

White
What color is the ambulance?
Black
Can you find a **black** scooter?

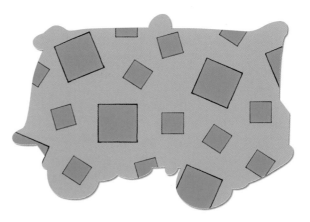

3

Mixing colors

Look at these smart children mixing paint! They are mixing their very own colors.

Blue and yellow make green.
The children are helping Huckle mix paint. Can you find the stickers that make the color **green**?

Red and white make pink.
Can you find the sticker with the children mixing **pink** paint?

Yellow and red make orange.
Can you find the **orange** paint sticker?

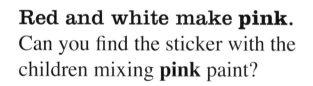

Oh-oh, Vincent is painting Papa's coat! Oh, dear!

Blue and red make purple.
Can you find the sticker with children mixing **purple** paint?

What a great painting of a fire engine! Aren't they smart children!

What a lot of colors there are!

Black and white make gray.
Look at those children helping to mix paint for the train. They are very helpful! Can you find the stickers that make the color **gray**?

Lots of shapes

Shapes can be found in everything.
Do you know your shapes?
Of course you do!

Square
What shape is Huckle Cat holding over his head?

Circle
What shape is Squeaky Mouse looking at?

Star
What shape is Sally Cat holding?

Oval
Can you see an **oval**?

Rectangle
What shape are the two bugs holding?

Cone
What shape is Lowly Worm wrapped around?

Triangle
Can you find a **triangle**?

Diamond
What shape is Huckle Cat holding?

My picture will have lots of shapes!

Cubes
Can you see any **cubes**? How many?

Cylinder
What shape is Huckle's disguise?

Finding shapes

What shape can you see in the middle of the playing field?

Can you see three **rectangles**?

Can you see four **round** wheels?

Can you see any **triangles** on the lake today?

Look at all those black and white shapes! What shapes are they?

Can you see a **diamond** in the sky?

What shape is the flag that Greenbug is holding?

Can you see a **round** ball?

Counting from 1 to 10

Numbers are for counting. Counting can be fun! Can you count to ten? Of course you can!

One

Two

Three

Four

Five

Six

Seven

Eight

Nine

Ten

1 one
Can you count **one** good pig brushing his teeth?

2 two
How many wet sponges are on the floor?

3 three

Three little hungry pigs are waiting for breakfast. How many flying eggs can you count?

4 four

How many pieces of toast are flying?

5 five

Clang! Clang! Clang! From the school bus Huckle can see **five** fire engines speed by.

6 six

How many children are riding in the school bus?

7 seven

How many airplanes are flying in the sky? That's right … **seven**!

8 eight

Wow! Look at all those speedboats! How many are out today?

9 nine

Look out, grumpy pigs! Here come **nine** mouse buggies.
What else can you count nine of?

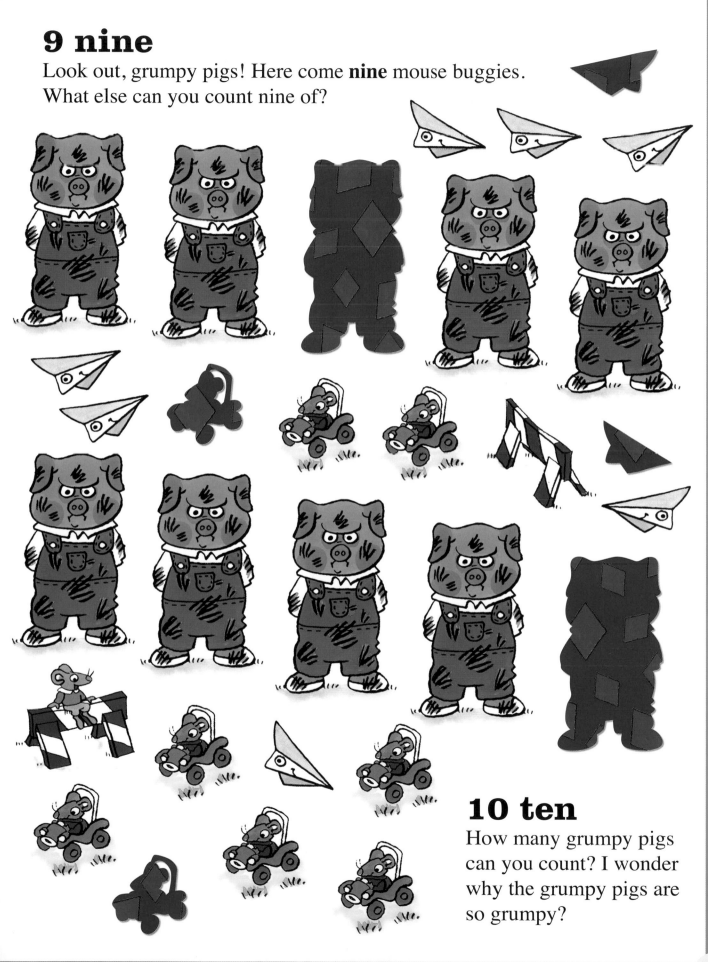

10 ten

How many grumpy pigs
can you count? I wonder
why the grumpy pigs are
so grumpy?

15

I know my colors, shapes, and numbers!

What **color** are the apples?
What **shape** are the eggs?
Can you **count** all the food the children are eating?

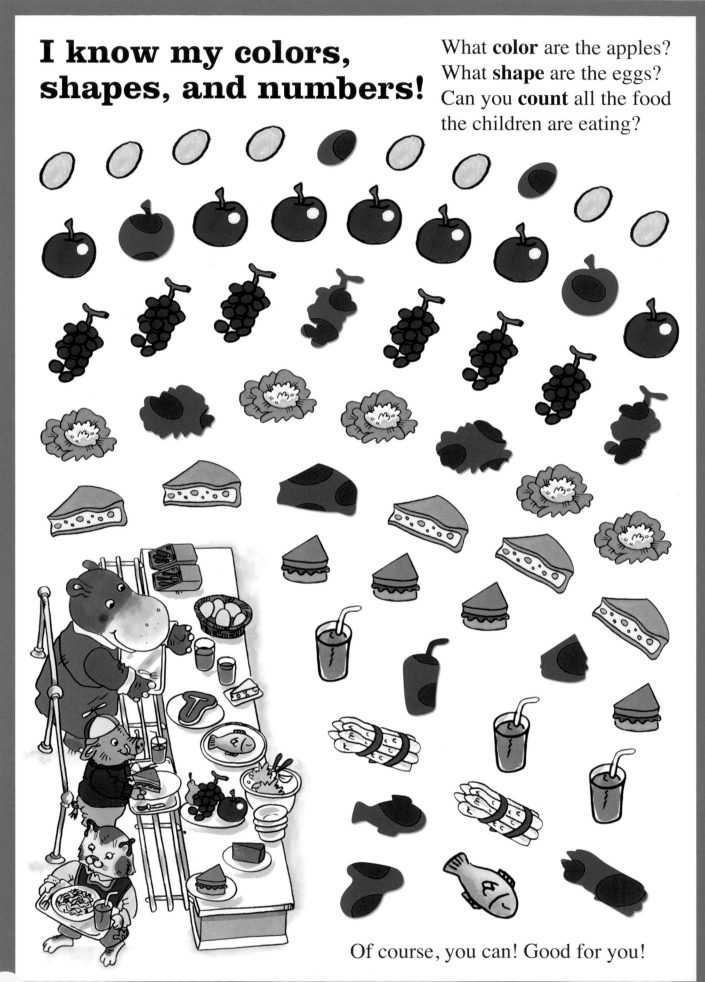

Of course, you can! Good for you!

Poster Stickers

1 2 3
4 5 6
7 8 9
10

More Stickers ... for you!
Decorate your lunch box, pencil case –
whatever you like!

My name is

My name is

This belongs to

My name is

This belongs to

Book Stickers